The Kingdom of Farfelu

with

Paper Moons

Fantôme de Napoléon III

The Kingdom of Farfelu

with

Paper Moons

by

André Malraux

Translated from the French by W.B. Keckler
Illustrations by André Malraux

fugue state press
new york

Royaume-farfelu © Éditions GALLIMARD, Paris, 1928
Lunes en papier © Éditions GALLIMARD, Paris, 1989

English translation Copyright © 2005 by W.B. Keckler

Library of Congress Control Number 2005925696
ISBN 1-879193-13-2

Back cover and text illustrations by André Malraux,
from *Messages, Signes, & Dyables*
© 1986 by Madeline Malraux and J. Damase,
reprinted by permission.

Our thanks to Madeline Malraux and Florence Giry
for their kind assistance.

Manufactured in the United States of America.

Published by Fugue State Press
PO Box 80, Cooper Station
New York NY 10276

www.fuguestatepress.com
info@fuguestatepress.com

PAPER MOONS

[1921]

*A small book in which one learns
of several little-known conflicts,
and a voyage among objects familiar but strange,
all of it true.*

To Max Jacob.

"Be careful, said the goldsmith, because you're dealing with some rather odd people here."

—Hoffmann, *Choosing a Fiancée*

Note: There are no symbols in this book.

PAPER MOONS

Prologue

Like a luminous advertising sign, the yellow moon changed color in phases: it turned red, then blue, green, then—ding!—yellow again. A piercing musical note dropped like a tiny frog, and opalescent vistas born in the play of light and water stretched over the lake surface to infinity.

A cork that floated on the lake turned into a box of surprises: a bearded man from Auvergne emerged from it and flew off, heedless of the two wakes he'd left forking on the water like hands on a clock face. Who was this sorcerer, whose birth glassed the lake surface and made the poor fountains abandon their circle dance? The moon herself didn't know. Little she cared, anyway: she was laughing. She laughed so hard that her notes, which were her teeth actually, came unhooked and fell through space. Teeth fluttered across the night like fattened stars, leaving fading streaks of luminescence, even as the notes touched down and opened, to the chiming of bells, the way paper flowers unfurl when you throw them on the water, and they surrounded the fearful and ironic eyes of the moon's tiny children. These newborns at first noticed only ominous balloons that rolled softly to and fro, like a harem of smooth, hairless, roly-poly sultans. The children of the moon, quite young, thought these balloons were carrying out complicated, invisible duties. When they realized the truth, they were indignant: their noses turned into billiard cues, and knocked the balloons out to the middle of the lake. Though fat, these balloons were so light that they just bounced around on the water. Their harmonious elegance inflamed the jealousy of the baby moons, who wanted them dead.

This wish was not to be granted. Since they could no longer just lounge, the balloons found themselves, alas, forced to act. They gazed about themselves languorously. The enchanted fountain drew itself up into a flickering amber palace, so perforated with windows that the walls looked like latticework. "In that palace we could commit all kinds of lovely infamy," the balloons murmured, and they decided to invade it. So one of the balloons rolled forward and began reading aloud a "position paper" it had written in high school. The contemptuous palace didn't respond at all...but this disdain would turn out to be fatal! The balloon kept reading—and at the word "Curtain!" the palace was suddenly lost in sleep. All the balloons bounced forward, each making for a different window, and they got inside with no trouble.

Once inside the palace they searched for the inhabitants, and found them all hanging from the crossbeams beneath the roof. It turned out they had fastened themselves there to escape the merciless beatings they'd all received at their various fair booths. Puppets of all kinds: glove puppets, gendarmes, rural policemen, newlyweds, devils, rustics with red umbrellas, concierges, characters from folk songs, all had come to the castle to form together this intricate mosaic. Now the savage balloons tied them all up, hand and foot, and stuck them on the windowsills: puppets were visible in every single window. The whole palace seemed to be waiting for a parade to come by, thanks to these strange faces brushed with yellow sulfur by the moon. Finally the perverse balloons attacked the puppets with smaller balloons—which were their children—as well as with black radishes full of sound (philosophers they'd found brooding on the crossbeams). The puppets all fell with a clicking sound.

While these strange things were happening, the genie of the lake, who was a cat-shaped pincushion, slept on. The tip of his tail traced in the sand a caricature of the fattest balloon. Suddenly he woke up and stared at the balloons—they had taken refuge on the high beams, their necks coiled around the wood. They jeered at him and howled like monkeys.

He stretched. Supple and distinguished, he gracefully posed his curving tail, pulled a keg up from a hole in the earth and drank from it, licking his chops.

As soon as he left, the spheres cork-screwed down like children down a greased pole. One by one they approached the keg. Since there was such a throng of them, the ones in the rear had to draw themselves up just to get a glimpse. Some of them thought the keg was full of explosives; others, without committing themselves to an opinion, nodded their heads anyway. Then one balloon that was famous for its courage dared to prod the keg gingerly with its neck. The agreeable aroma encouraged the balloon to suck up a bit of the liquid inside—it was a fine vintage champagne!

Madly the balloons rushed the keg. They were beautiful as they struggled, like grapes clustering! Several of them were killed in the stampede, and deflated pitifully. Finally, when the others decided it was time to return to their perches high in the beams, they suddenly realized they were not quite as dignified and serious as they should be. They were reeling, completely drunk!

They stretched out on the ground and fell deep asleep.

On mincing feet the cat returned. He snickered. He gathered the balloons by their necks, grapes in a bunch, and tied them together so they couldn't escape.

"Hello! Hello everybody! Just look at these splendid balloon prisoners! I'm not even selling these beauties today; I'm *giving* them away. What? No one wants even one of these things? Excuse me? O Ancient Night, are you suggesting that since there are no balloon aficionados around here, I'll never be able to get rid of these? I refuse to listen to such nonsense!

"Since no one desires these cruel balloons, We, the Genie of the Lake, who possess rights of justice, high and low, over the totality of this, Our Fiefdom, condemn these balloons to death in the name of justice. They shall all hang.

"Ah—and you once told me I'm the type who just *lives* to see balloons with their tongues hanging out, really suffering! According to you, all my life I've followed low passions like this, and I'm a true specimen of a Tomcat Deluxe! But you also said I would never capture you! So? What do you say now?"

The balloons said nothing, because they

were all dead drunk.

"No one's coming to rescue you. This morning I heard the sound of ocarinas welded to boulders, moaning 'Assassins! Assassins!' I snuck up on them, and poisoned them with parsley.

"Now to untie you. Okay, done—which of you is going to be first? I think I'll start with this fatso here. First we separate him from the other balloons. Then we throw him over our back like a sack. God, how useful this long neck is! Fine. Now, we're heading way up there to the top of the palace.

"You see this slipknot, my chubby little balloon? Don't you want me to make it into a necklace for you? No? I see: you are one of those forever insensitive to beauty. Good thing I'm here to guide you in these aesthetic matters! But there's no time to waste now on irony or games of patience: let's tie the end of the rope to this crossbeam. Perfect! And now...

WE LET YOU DROP

JUST LIKE THIS!

Now to dash back downstairs!"

As soon as he was back on the lakebed, he posed like a sphinx, then lifted his head to look.

"What? But...but...but...that balloon's been hanged, and he won't stick out his tongue! No doubt about it, his tongue's still *completely inside his head*! He refuses to let it out! Is he too lightweight to really stretch the rope, is that it? Salmagundi! We'll see about this!"

Furious, he rounded up the scattered balloons and, dragging them all along, climbed back up inside the castle. And he hung these balloons too, noosed into a long line, one after another, to increase the weight; then he climbed down again.

"What a gorgeous rosary! I always knew I was a true artist. But...are they really dead? Good Christ! Their tongues are still playing hide and seek! They're really stubborn!

"Obstinacy! My life is a failure, irremediable! O passion, you're about to lose your little Cat Deluxe!"

And so the cat, too, hung himself...his neck noosed at the very end of the rosary of balloons, and his paws laid fittingly across each other in the shape of a cross.

And his weight did the trick. The rope at last came taut; each of the grapelike spheres stuck out its tongue in turn. Then that amulet attached to the end—which was a cat with paws crossed on his chest—ejected a triumphant tongue that seemed to want to lash all the others, but then fell back flaccid, as if burst by a pin.

Dyable de l'investigation

I. Combat

May somebody chop off your head with a jack-straw. —Sigogne.

Some of the balloons blossomed into huge flowers, their fringed petals covered with a deep-red fluff that the wind set shivering. The tickling stirred the flowers to laughter that rang out like doorchimes. Maybe somebody blew on their pistils, because they unfolded and flew up the nose of the wind, and the wind ran off guffawing.

Other balloons had metamorphosed into fruits with the soft gleam of antique polished wood; the oldest of these globes looked like giant mushrooms held above the ground by fat extruding nodules.

They gave off a strange odor. Stuffed alligators ran out of antique shops on their short little legs, drawn by the aphrodisiac aroma. The alligators arrived Indian file among the balloons, and flung themselves into a dance, a pavane, following each other's tails, keeping perfect rhythm. Their sharp pointy tails marked the land in rows, dotted lines of perfect regularity. Maybe the alligators would have liked to tear open these big chunks of dotted earth (like the perforated notecards they now resembled), despite the sealing wax of phosphorescent mushrooms. But the alligators never expressed such a desire. Several of them, who had been poorly stuffed, lost their straw and died slowly; some others with more minor wounds remained off to the side, carefully tending their injuries with white silk bandages.

Suddenly one of the fruits burst open. Like spores, nine new beings went flying out, flipping nine of the alligators onto their backs and leaving them on the ground like bowling pins. The nine beings hid in nearby hedges, then met back up with each other They lay down in the shade of cone-shaped trees from which seemed to hang...were they amulets? fetishes? dangling fruit? Actually they were big scarlet apples, which were in fact hearts. Of these nine beings, seven were white, and on their chests and backs they each bore, like an insect carapace, an ancient fool's scepter with carved Capuchin head. Tall stiff cotton caps rose on their heads like the hair of terrified people, and their pompoms turned in the wind, now left, now right, like the faces of passionate preachers. The two other beings were red: the first one's nose was too pointy, like it had got stuck in a bottleneck; the second one's eyes were like snail's eyes, held up on two erect peduncles.

Two of the white beings, the two smallest, exploded. And then, slowly, the largest one stood up to speak.

"Gentlemen," he said to the two red beings, "the absence of previous acquaintance obliges me to perform a few introductions."

And, pointing to his companions:

"A bevy of sins: Anger, Lust, Gluttony, Sloth. I am Pride. A few moments ago you saw Envy and Greed expire, quite exhausted."

He lay down again.

"Gentlemen," replied the red Pinocchio, "forgive me for not getting up. My introduction will take a little longer than yours—I'm still feeling a bit unsteady, and I'm not in any rush to perish by exploding.

"My name is Hifili. Before the metamorphoses that gave me this balloon soul, I was a man who carefully studied shapes. It started with my love of chemical glassware, which I quickly learned to tame.

"Ignoring the flasks, I lived among the retorts, the balloons and the tubing. I loved the retorts most of all. I had enormous and tiny ones, potbellied and slender ones. I knew them all intimately and they all knew me. If I called, they came hopping. They would have run to eat out of my hand if they had known how to eat. These vessels are often maligned, you know. Crass men claim that retorts are always pregnant, which is nonsense. Lewd women are drawn to that glass phallus. The retorts would laugh at all this— contemptuous laughter, because retorts are sardonic—and then would stick their necks out from their swollen bellies as a sight gag. They take vengeance on those who dare to displease them by appearing in their dreams, improbable beaks open and eyes on fire. I cannot initiate you completely into my science, gentlemen. But just realize that retorts express friendship by strange acts you will probably soon experience—and they show their affection by an amazing expansion."

He added, but now in a deep muffled

voice, attractively sly:

"I am the master of glass."

"Gentlemen," said the second red being, "my story, though not as pretty as the one you've just heard, is almost as unusual. Before I had the mind of a balloon, I was a musician. One day, down at the end of the street, I saw about fifty small rods all hopping up and down like bobbins. Threads were coming off them, and an immense translucent lace seemed to be forming in the air around me. I admired its subtlety, I touched it, but then realized I was trapped in its net. This lace was a cage! Just seconds after I'd been wrapped in this material, the size of my chest doubled; the trunk of my body had been replaced with a mandolin! Immediately I tried some chords: they sounded sour, gentlemen, out of tune! Can you imagine my despair? Out of tune! And it was impossible to correct them, because the tuning pegs and the neck of the mandolin were hidden inside my head!"

"Those are fine résumés, gentlemen," said Pride, "and I'm happy to know you. May I ask, what are your future plans?"

Dead silence.

"Alas, your plans may not be sufficiently thought-out. May I make a suggestion? You have the advantage of only ever having lived in a text; you are imaginary. This makes you qualified to replace our two dead colleagues—would you be interested? Being a mortal sin can not only give your life a purpose, but is also a career with many attractive benefits."

The two red beings consulted with each other. Then the musician seized one of the buttons on Pride's suit and, tugging it a little with each gesture, said:

"We accept, sir. We accept for a number of reasons. You will never know them all."

Pride made a gesture, as much to save himself having to reply as for politeness, a gesture meaning anything.

"You will only know one reason," continued the musician, "and that's enough: if we didn't accept your offer, we would end up in a lot of trouble."

Pride accepted this silently. But he considered the response gauche, and felt quite proud to be a born mortal sin, sensitive to such nuances. He wished he were wearing a frock coat—since a coat like that always makes such a serious impression—and he replied:

"Fine."

Immediately the two red beings lost all color and began to look just like the other sins.

"Gentlemen, I presume you know God?"

"I used to know him," replied Hifili, "he's a nice old guy."

"Nice guy, yes, but a little vulgar," qualified the musician.

"And how can he help being vulgar? He mingles with so many people, and so many people know him, even today!"

"He's no longer vulgar," said Pride. "As he's aged, he has become completely oblivious. He's already changed his name and his uniform countless times, without attaching any importance to it—so Satan, who isn't stupid, has taken his place this time, and neither God nor anyone else noticed it. But since Satan has taken over for God, we could take over for Satan. What do you think?"

"Our authority would be almost nil," declared Anger. "Satan's best ally, Death, will destroy us."

"I've already thought of that. It's no problem at all. We'll just kill Death!"

Hifili was so thrilled with this idea that he jumped around in manic ecstasy. His nose-protector fell off, and he picked it up and pushed it back on with a painful grunt.

Flashes of light tormented the trees. From far off, the spiky treetops seemed like random shapes, but as the pale beings entered the forest they saw that the low-hanging leaves made geometric patterns: spheres, cubes, prisms, and each pattern had a luminous core, like the bright eye of an ironic Russian hare.

A rosary of lightning-bolts. The sins, all alert, saw a cable coming out of an airhole at the very top of the rosary. They watched as it pierced some solid forms without bursting them, the way a needle pierces taut skin, leaving perfectly drilled holes through which the wind whistled. A necklace of hearts like this, which had already been threaded together, Death now wore around her neck. Death had refinished the hearts' silky surface with a japanned glaze, and they swelled like reddest pimientos.

"Look who's grown curious," said Hifili.

Each time a heart was punctured, its point bled a little, but soon clotted shut, and a long stem oozed out of it like a soap bubble from a pipe and fell and rooted in the ground. Although there was no sunlight, these stems glowed. New stems fell like a storm of darts, and began to thicken into groves of thistles.

No birds flew through these woods; only kangaroos, those fat windbags, jumped around, disgracefully clumsy, pitifully trying to get inside this growing forest of pricks. One of the largest cut himself when he tried to jump at the wrong moment into an opening in the huge thicket; he fell back whimpering, several of the stems lodged in his body like banderillas. He managed to get away, a porcupine now. The wind, thinking itself a musician, made the stems jangle all along his body, and even curled the tufts of moss he had caught on himself into treble clefs.

"Stranger and stranger," said a pale little sin.

"Quiet!"

Then a metamorphosis: the little darts that had seemed to be mere red beribboned larding-needles were by now a mass of stalks.

They shed their leaves, and merged to form a parallelepiped the size of a tower. The cable, having finally gathered up all the hearts, wound itself around and rose up playfully on its tail like a trained serpent. A regrettable lapse! The thread of the necklace broke, and the cunning hearts took off. The cable, wanting to snatch them up again, shot out, but they disappeared in all directions like a whirlwind of plump little cupids with their bottoms spanked red.

"See, my friends!" said Pride. "Scarcely have we made our plans than Death tries to destroy us. She's completely wrong, of course. And her methods are so vulgar. Did you know these hearts are potentially explosive?"

"What? I had no idea!" said Gluttony. "Maybe we should take some precautions?"

"No point," said ingenious Hifili. "Because Death has an impoverished imagination. You'll see."

He pulled two little glass tongs from his pocket, and threw them in the air. They lifted softly like paper butterflies, the toy ones driven by a rubber band. On reaching the cable, they grabbed it by the ends and made it spin like a little girl's jump rope. Now the sins could only see a sparkling ball, like the rotating mirrors used to catch larks. In the distance, dark specks appeared, then drew closer... One by one, fascinated, the hearts flew into the ball. It knocked them all senseless.

Hifili whistled. The tongs returned; the cable fell limply back to earth. All the sins came and studied the unconscious hearts. When they had enough of studying them, they lit them by the pointy end. Since there were so many, they had to use the kind of match that keeps burning like a candle; luckily, Sloth had brought some along.

When a heart was almost burnt up, a huge flame spurted from it, drawing broken patterns on the air like Greek vase paintings, ripping open the atmosphere. Each pattern as it broke apart blossomed into a large motionless jellyfish of light.

"Now on to Death's empire!" said Lust.

Pride protested: "Sir—please don't make us look ridiculous with statements like that. Everyone knows that 'Death's empire' is called the Kingdom of Farfelu."

And the sins set out for the Kingdom of

Farfelu. They went without looking back, and so missed the pleasure of watching those jellyfish of light descending like parachutes and delicately winking out.

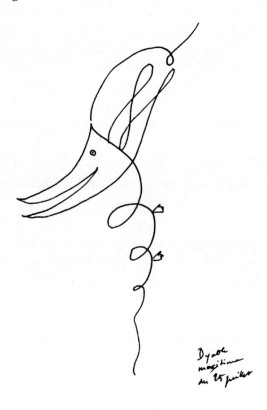

II. Voyages

The positions change once more. —Sade.

The sins had no interest in acts that could be performed by just anyone. Besides, the proper use of feet eluded them. So they walked on their hands toward the river that led to the Kingdom of Farfelu. Thus they marked the landscape with strange asterisks and unknown punctuation marks. And they were delighted with themselves, because they saw how much Creation is in need of touching up, and how much more harmonious it could all be through the contributions of Sin.

The evening was completely blue. On the backs of the sins, the dark scepters now dehisced and began to phosphoresce, a pale gray light. Hifili, metamorphosed into Greed now, watched the sins all brighten. He was ecstatic. To see these spidery backs transformed into captured stars stirred him. He felt he could accept the sins as his true friends. Now he would be able to look at them in the daylight without the disgust he'd always felt for anything resembling a wingless insect. And he walked on, turning over in his head a puzzle, pieces of a fairy tale in which millipedes, transformed into immense luminous ferns, beat the air like palm leaves and voluptuously rocked harems of stars.

His companions stopped. His reverie fell from him like a mask: he was facing the river. Tufts of fur floated in the fast current; the pale beings wanted to plunge their arms up to the armpits into this vegetation, which was so much like sumptuous red pelts, and stay like that for hours, their eyes shut, motionless, just feeling the gorgeous caresses. An animal musk, intoxicating as ether, rose from these fur tufts; when a sin breathed it, he felt that fruits of the flesh were against his lips, that he took a bite, and that the fruits were bursting open, splattering all across his face their sugared blood.

A red halo in the air surrounded the small floating islands of fur. These were small horned birds with palm-leaf wings, who made so much noise in flight that long after they disappeared the sins still heard the fading chatter of a thousand castanets. One bird had perched on the shoulder of Gluttony. Its long, slender tail was prickly with hair, its skin was orange velvet, except for two black rings around its eyes like eyeglass frames. It flew off.

Birds were so thick around the fur tufts that many of them, leaving their places in the halo for a moment, were unable to crowd back in. These birds hovered awhile above the river and then, one by one, fell in. Purple circles began to grow on the water...and in their centers grew a round iridescence of gilded lacquerwork, which opened like an expanding eye.

So many birds were falling in and so much gold glazed the river's surface that soon it was a blonde head of hair, its reflections moving and changing constantly. Surely underwater hands caressed it. The briskness of the air became pure cold. Since sins are beings, not creatures, they had the luxury of passing the night out of doors, but they did miss their accustomed comforts. So when they reached the next town they entered an inn.

The innkeeper, dressed in a black smock and apron, removed his black cap and asked: "In which room could you gentlemen pass with the least misery the beginning of the rest of your poor lives?" Together the sins visited each room and quickly chose one lit by a full window and two dormers, large enough that they could all stay together. Then they lay down and fell asleep.

Upstairs, a phonograph was trying to overcome its unfortunate case of laryngitis.

After an hour, Pride was awakened by disturbing sounds, like delicate glass clocks being bumped into. He scanned the room. Gangs of mice and voles were scuttling through the room. They were gold, and as they passed they left bright traces in the darkness. Weary with life, they bumped into each other constantly as they busily gathered up bells. Sitting on the handrail were two rats pink as coral; they washed and groomed themselves with their claws, and composed elegies of love.

"My god," said Pride, "maybe I'm seeing things." He wanted to wake his companions, but he found only four of them. Lust had run off with the musician, and their silhouette against the window, their legs obscenely wrapped around each other, divided the night sky into two unequal crescents. "She's so indecent," Pride sputtered. "How handy for her to be a sin, so she can behave so coldly. Besides, come on! Her current sex, which is male, must pose a problem for her young man—he might not be up for the rear door. He has actually become Envy, hasn't he. It's all food for thought. When I have time, I'll have to consider it in more depth."

The sins grumbled.

"Hey, Pride! Are you going to turn on the lights or what? We can't see a thing!"

"Don't you have a candle, idiot?"

"No, I only have matches, ordinary matches."

"Then let us go back to sleep!"

"Wait. I've got an idea."

He took the hat Lust had left lying there and lit the tassel. It burned with a lovely, unprecedented flame. The mice, voles and rats scattered, but coils appeared in each corner of the room, and soon they unrolled into snakes.

"What's that?" whispered Gluttony. "Do you think it's Death, launching an attack of snakes? Look at them—filthy creatures, and in such bad taste. Besides, what harm can snakes do to immortals? This tactic is ridiculous."

But the largest snake reared up and

towered over them, balancing on the tip of its tail, saying:

"Idiots. You confuse us with snakes! Snakes yourselves! To those in the know, we are quite respectable, upright—and dangerous. We are Bigophones."

And the sins grew fearful. Even without knowing why, they understood that great and tragic events loomed ahead.

"We know by heart a number of banal poems and stupid songs, too frightful to even imagine. We're about to sing them to you, one after another. Our famous nasality will make them particularly exasperating. Within ten minutes you will flee; if not, you will go completely mad. We will drive you to the very edge of the Kingdom of Farfelu.

"You smirk? You're wrong—you're completely wrong to think your past experience has made you immune. Even if you withstood us, we would call on the help of our friends the Bigophone Ducks, the Bigophone Hunting Horns, the Bigophone Bugles, the Bigophone Trumpets, the Bigophone Baby Bottles, the Bigophone Dolphins, the Bigophone Clarinets, the Bigophone Adders and the Bigophone Sausages. And you'd run like hell, my little gargoyles, to get away from these heedless Graces!"

"What crap!"

The words rang like hammerstrokes on the nose of silence. It was the musician. He'd just entered, holding in his right hand the phonograph horn.

"I wrung the neck of this bird," he continued; "it had no sense of harmony. My dear Bigophones, do you know what's special about these horns?"

Disdainfully, the snakes began singing a terrible popular tune. Already some of the sins looked disturbed, but only a moment later the musician put the phonograph horn to his lips and blew, and mournful sounds issued from it: the snakes stared at him. As soon as they set eyes on this horn they couldn't look away. They were mesmerized. The musician led them outside into the courtyard; he took a ladder, climbed it, found a hook attached to the lattice ceiling. He hung the horn there like a bell; it swung back and forth, then came slowly to a standstill. And the Bigophone Snakes went rigid, stared at the horn as if they were a squadron placed there just to guard it.

"Good! Just stay there, my little friends. Stay that way as long as you can. You may get tired, but I'd hate to break up this weird tableau—it's worthy of interest to any passing artist. Besides, think of the education you're getting! Ah, if only you'd been taught common sense…"

He ran back to find his friends again.

"What's up?"

"Nothing. But…well, listen: right after you left, Lust came back in and told us that, because of her bashfulness, she could return only when you weren't here. She was punished for that lie— she was concentrating so hard on what she was saying, she didn't see the burning hat, and got scorched by it."

"That's fine by me. Anything else?"

"A few minutes later, we thought we heard strange noises coming from the stairs."

"Well, let's see," said the musician.

He went to the stairhead and leaned his elbows on the handrail.

"Oh! You've got to see this!"

Bizarre lightning flashes were slowly

floating upward, clown lightning no doubt, because the lights seemed all twisted, like a lovesick person's facetious nervous attacks. Looking closer, the sins recognized these lights as Geissler tubes. Deceptively lethargic, Geissler tubes are actually wicked and aggressive electric beasts, a constant menace. The sins quickly retreated to their room, but the tubes followed them. When the last tube had entered, the musician pulled a luminous phial from his pocket, took out a little lozenge of compressed electricity, and threw it on the floor.

It rolled like a billiard ball past one of the tubes, who snapped it up and instantly looked abnormally happy. He reared up his head; it made him resemble a strange microbe. Lust thought him handsome, and let him notice her appreciation. Suddenly the tube jumped up and fell to the floor. He seemed racked by great pain for a few seconds, then he leapt on his fellow tubes and gnawed them with his teeth.

He was rabid.

The tubes were all convulsing; they nearly blacked out. The sins took their opportunity to escape from the room and lock the door. They'd just thrown the last bolt when they heard a crash of shattering crystal, and their curiosity impelled them to look through the keyhole. They saw great shards of glass, swimming in a sea of blue light.

"Beautiful," said Pride. "But we sins have our own lives to pursue...so I think the safest thing would be to get out of here."

The sins linked arms and took off, each putting his left foot forward, because they liked to conjure up bad luck.

The day awoke. Thanks to the atmosphere, half the sky was covered with vast geometric flowers of rose-colored frost. A violet light filtered through them and covered everything. The sins walked along the course of the river, as they had the night before, and watched countless mauve egrets settle like little arrows on the pale reflecting water. After twenty minutes' travel, they saw the river was winding around an extremely rugged mountain; wanting to get as far away from the inn as they could, and as fast as possible, they took a shortcut that lay across the mountain like a metallic thread. As they walked along, a head would come out from under every rock. These heads were carved in pyramid shape, embellished with a coffeepot spout for a nose, with owl eyes, and pocketknife blades for ears. Sometimes the whole creature appeared and stretched itself out lengthwise, its body made up of an herb called the "oyster plant." Then it would stand up on its sparrow's feet and work its round flippers, which looked like those paper hoops that little pink pigs jump through at a clown's command. The sins, marching on, approached the top of the mountain. They heard a mewing sound and stopped dead. Immediately all the feather-legged oyster-plant creatures rushed at them.

*

When the innkeeper, who was a poet, came outside with his hands in his pockets to express to the morning some small desire to be a hero, he could just make out at the top of the mountain his lodgers of the night before, locked in a frantic, losing struggle. Their arms flailed regularly, and each time one of those windmills completed a revolution, an inhabitant of the mountain had its tail yanked off, and rose up shrieking into the sky, then, fluttering its small rounded wings, slowly descended.

And the innkeeper, who was a poet, thought he was watching a powder puff whose fragile feathers, carried off by the wind, fell delicately in every direction.

III. Victory

The town of Farfelu was celebrating: its queen, Death, was suffering a bout of listlessness, and she had requested all the doctors of the town to convene immediately to vote for the one doctor among them worthy of caring for Her Majesty. Unusually enough, when the previous Royal Doctor died, no successor had been named, despite the urging of the Chief of Protocol.

The doctors announced they would arrive in retinue at the Royal Palace at 4 p.m. Orders had been given that the town was to be decorated. Many citizens considered this a bother: they loved their homes, and were so used to their charm that they felt the facades of their houses were actually true faces like their own. Alas, now they had to apply pancake makeup, limewash and ripolin paint. Some citizens were running around upset because they'd made up the eyes of their houses, and now could hardly recognize their own sluttish windows.

The townspeople showed their love for their queen by hanging precious objects in the

windows. Crystal wineglasses on glowing threads
dangled everywhere in the weary afternoon
breeze; invisible small bells jingled for every
passerby. The windows of aristocrats showed
aristocratic spirit: silver renderings of buttercups
and bitter apple hung in wreaths, while busts of
dead humorists watched from the high corners of
the house. Around the eyepits of the sculpted
faces, a circle of white frost expressed the same
look of irony one sees in stuffed bears. The busts
were probably carved out of frozen champagne,
since, as they melted, golden drops fell one by one
onto the heads of the strollers below, as if a slap
in the face were made of light. The homes of
grand dignitaries had hollow glass spheres beside
their front doors; from time to time these spheres
rose into the air and played music, even began to
sing, holding passersby in thrall. And round,
smooth objects resembling the eyes in peacock
tails flew through the air like trapped swallows.
They kept high out of reach, knowing the strollers
wanted to catch them and pin them onto cork-
board. In fact most of these bourgeois collectors
were feeling irritated that day, because here they
were wearing their gold ceremonial hats for the

first time, and yet the gold was invisible under all the flying objects they'd caught and pinned onto the hats. The innumerable pins made their hats look like hedgehogs on their heads, very strange little hedgehogs whose prickles had blossomed with the flowers of sad eyes.

*

Death inhabited a chamber with immense mirrored walls, reproducing to infinity the furniture in the room. Her furniture seemed to be reddish eiderdown cushions of various sizes. Among them, Her Majesty resembled a giant insect, because of her dinner jacket. She wore it out of modesty, or perhaps from fear of the cold, and despite the perfection of its cut, it fluttered on her, and gave her wings in the breeze.

A valet entered. He looked old and wizened, but it's also possible that he was a fetus.

"The Royal Physician waits in attendance until it might please Your Highness bid him enter."

"It pleases me now."

He was immediately ushered in. He wore a

black frock with a yellow ribbon rosette, a mark of his dignity. His features were rather Japanese.

"Would Her Highness deign to disrobe?"

Death removed her dinner jacket and her slacks; two cushions, hopping up, snatched them and carried them off, walking on tiptoes.

"I've already had the very great honor of caring for Your Highness," began the doctor, "a long time ago. My predecessor, the Royal Physician, had retired to his country estate, and Your Highness, who suffered from a slight catarrh, had deigned to believe that my services might be of use to Her."

"Of course, of course! You and I are old acquaintances..."

"Had not Your Highness, back then, vertebrae in the Royal Back?"

"Yes, yes; but I have had them replaced with these, which are aluminum, and much more practical. The maintenance is so simple—after an hour of brisk polishing I am meticulously clean."

"What? Your Highness must make the Royal Toilet...Herself?"

"Oh, you know, I'm a good-natured queen. They always say *Death! Death!* Truth is, my soul is like a telegraph pole that's gone sentimental because it's transmitted too many love letters."

"And to tend to your own toilet, you find it as pleasant as when it was done for you in days of old?"

"As *pleasant*! Come off it! My dear man, you're making fun of me! To let them *polish* me is one thing—but they used to scrape away half my back!"

The doctor apologized for speaking in such a manner.

"This new skeleton," she said, "has turned out to be so much more elegant than the old one...just look, when the sunset strikes it..."

Death walked to the window: sunlight bounced around her thoracic cavity, and the aluminum glowed like red copper.

"A novel effect," agreed the physician.

"Isn't it? And the metal's so delicate, so light. Anyway, we must keep up with Progress. Everything has become mechanical, metallic, dazzling, and yet my beauty remained Gothic. I was slipping into the passé."

"And you have been able to create a skeleton entirely of aluminum?"

"No, alas! My joints—see here in my arm for instance—are brass."

"Brass! Ah! Brass! Amazing! Brass!"

"That surprises you?"

"Er...no, Highness, no—it uh...delights me... Yes, delightful! I mean the aesthetics of the thing. Your Highness would permit an auscultation?"

"Proceed."

And she bent over. The doctor gave a little tap to the aluminum and it echoed with a noise that might have come from a mechanical rabbit.

"The ceremony," continued Death. "Tell me, did you find it pleasant?"

"Impressive, Highness. The procession, above all."

"I didn't see that. You had everyone dress in the ceremonial costume?"

"Yes, Highness. Balaclava helmets in the form of Chinese lanterns, with black robes and illuminated cigars."

The doctor finished auscultating Death and said gravely:

"I will not allow myself to hide the seriousness of the Royal Condition from Your Highness.

If I had not been able to examine the Royal Body today, Your Highness would have suffered numerous terrible maladies, the least of which—baldness—would have taken a great toll on the beauty of Your Highness."

"Oh God! To lose my hair! My most precious ornament! You're seriously scaring me! You know a remedy, at least?"

"Your Highness can only be saved by bathing five times a day in a special liquid, of which I alone know the formula. If Your Highness permits, I will prepare the bath and…"

"How soon can I take my first bath in this liquid?"

"When it please Your Highness."

"As soon as possible. I mean, to lose my hair!"

"It will suffice me one hour to prepare the solution. If Your Highness would be so kind as to leave standing orders that no one is to enter this chamber?"

"Fine."

Death rang. The fetus returned.

"The key to this chamber?"

It was in his pocket. He handed it over to

Death and withdrew.

"Here is the key, Doctor. Use it as you see fit. What time is it?"

"Seven o'clock, Highness."

"At eight I'll be back here."

And she exited.

Then, six of the cushions burst without a sound. Six sins emerged from them and surrounded the doctor, who took a handkerchief and wiped the features off his face as if it were only makeup. He revealed himself to be the seventh sin: Pride.

"What are you going to do now?" asked Hifili.

"Mix her a bath of nitric acid; her joints will dissolve and we'll each pull out one of her bones. That way she will be destroyed forever."

"But she'll feel the burning, and she'll realize that..."

"You're wrong. You're such a young sin, you don't realize—*she is completely numb, without feelings.*"

"But she'll *see* the effects of the acid!"

"Do you think I'm stupid? I'll prepare the acid so it's no more transparent than milk."

"Then we've got everything covered, and…"

"And enough! Get back into hiding. I'm going to call some unsuspecting servants to come and assist me…and soon…"

"Dear friend," the musician intervened, "no melodrama, please. A sin owes it to himself not to act as his title suggests. Even the various loves of Lust were only chimeras, and didn't last."

Pride looked at him sullenly, jealous of the musician's intelligence.

*

Death's black coif, curly as the pelt of a poodle, stuck up above the porcelain tub rim. She was letting the blissful warmth of the bath penetrate when her lady servant Rifloire ran panic-stricken into the chamber.

"Get out of the tub!"

Death didn't stir an inch.

"Out of the tub, I said! You're being poisoned!"

"Oh lord, my dear girl," said Death, "you have such beautiful shoulders."

Rifloire, who also had false bones (but only a celluloid skeleton—although poor, she had pure motives, and had never accepted gifts from her queen)—Rifloire, who was bald despite her youth—collapsed, her legs splayed out like calipers.

"You don't get it? You've been poisoned!"

"Poisoned isn't exactly the right word. I am being corroded."

The cushions stirred.

"And you're just lying there!"

"Yes, obviously. You see, I would never have been able to commit suicide. How thankful I am, what a debt I owe to whoever helped me out of this sorrow."

"Huh?!"

"Yes, dear friend, I've had enough. The world (it's useless to stand there gaping—I'll soon be dead), the world is only tolerable to us because of our habit of tolerating it. They inflict this tolerance on us when we're still too young to resist, and then...do you see what I mean? If we can suppress the habit of—"

"I don't understand..."

"Well, it's not hard to figure out! Let's say

your friends are eggcups, for example. Can't you see them handing out, at random, the title of God of the Eggcups, and confiding to him their eggcup desires? Can't you imagine the female eggcups saying with a smirk 'The balance and harmony of the female eggcup is clearly superior to that of the male eggcup'? My god, just look at them all! I've had enough of the whole game, I tell you, enough! I'm ill and you're trying to pick a fight with me— well, I'm taking my umbrella and leaving. My departure will be a great practical joke. They call me Death but you know perfectly well that I'm only Chance. Slow decay is just one of my dis- guises. But, now, where's she gone? Rifloire! Rifloire! She took off! The slut! Whore! Well... finally! I've been a torment to her, and now that I'm going to die she won't be able to even take revenge upon me. Oh, let's get it over with!"

And she lit a cigarette. A sinuosity of smoke rose like a delicate, wispy girl floating on the air, and Death tried to imagine all sorts of pornographic shapes, tried to will them into movements that would correspond to the swaying of the thread of smoke.

And not a single cushion stirred.

*

Death was dead. Sitting on the battlements of the highest castle tower, the sins watched evening soothe the peaceful town. No change was yet visible.

"And now, back to work!" said Pride.

"To work!" repeated the other sins.

"Where should we start?" asked Hifili.

A long pause. Then the musician spoke, hesitantly:

"Forgive me, dear friends... When I was a man, I was subject to a kind of mental anemia. So please don't mind too much if I ask: Why, exactly, did we kill Death?"

The sins had hung pieces of her skeleton from their belts like scalps or trophies. They rubbed them between their fingers and repeated:

"Yes, why *did* we kill Death?"

They looked at each other with mournful faces. Then they put their heads into their hands and wept. Why had they killed Death? They had completely forgotten.

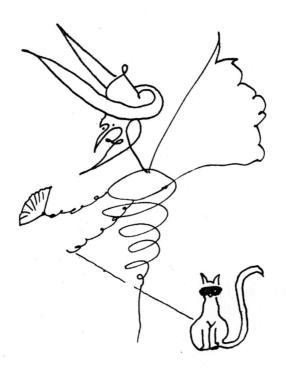

Dyall estrèmement vénétien
Le 1er 6er 46

ROYAUME-FARFELU

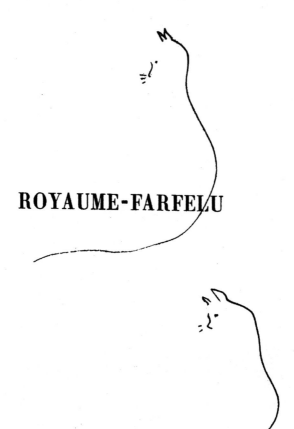

THE KINGDOM
OF FARFELU

[1928]

THE KINGDOM
OF FARFELU

Watch out, curlyhaired devils: ghost images are forming on the silent sea. This hour no longer belongs to you. Look, look: across from sanctified tombs, night watchmen climb slowly into clocks that measure out eternity in the form of dead sultans. Gilded popes and antipopes walk along the empty gutters of Rome; behind them, demons with silken tails—who are former emperors—laugh mutely. A vagabond walks through the desert toward a dazzling city, surrounded by occasional volleys of startled partridges; when evening comes, the partridges huddle around him like chicks. A king, who no longer cares for

anything but music and the art of torture, wan-
ders the night disconsolate, blowing on upraised
silver trumpets, leading his dancing subjects
onward. And see, beyond the two Indies, under
trees with leaves that seem the sharp talons of
beasts, a broken conqueror sleeps in black armor,
surrounded by restless monkeys...

Then with a great jingling of bells, the
beings who were tormenting us flew away, carrying off with them our ship's sails. This black
squadron of devils, all spiky with horns, got
smaller, smaller, and finally was swallowed up in
the intense frozen moonlight. The current carried
us on toward the coast in silence. Across the
smooth water bit by bit a town appeared, with
architecture that looked barely human. Shadows
thronged the shore; the largest were wearing
voluminous turbans of silk brocade. They were
Turks in long black beards, and looked like
Charlemagne. Bluish shadows out of the night's
blue phosphorescence—Turks—a sudden flight of
devils—and this village with its improbable
skyline evoking crustaceans and mushrooms...

Merchants threw themselves on us as soon
as we touched land. One of them, a phoenix-

vendor, incinerated one of those creatures before our eyes. The phoenix was reborn immediately from its ashes, but then took advantage of the merchant's foolhardy joy and escaped, flapping off in heavy graceless flight. Dismay. Everyone looked up, everyone followed the phoenix's retreat; nothing in the silence except distant voices crying: "Oh city born of the sea, one day the fish of darkness will invade your animal-shaped palaces…"

"And me, I sell dragons. They are immortal, and so beautiful that mere contemplation of them overcomes the worst suffering, the most poignant sorrow. They can also be used as barometers; when the crest on their backs is erect, then rain is coming. Sometimes they give good advice too. And I buy them in their native country… I also sell this gloomy fish, whose only amusement is to light up each of its eyes in turn, red or white light according to the time of day. Its habits gave rise to the fable of the Sirens, because it inhabits only those shipwrecks that still hold great treasures. Among pearls adding opalescence to the sea, among forgotten green glimmering coins, among clustered jewels scattered by giant crabs, this fish swims, wearing lightly its title: King of Swallowed Riches…"

Jostled by crowds, I passed sidewalk displays: trays full of orange eggs, rose-colored lime and leaves, tattooed ducks, dehydrated rats translucent as gray jade and tied by their tails into bouquets, trays full of oblong tortoiseshells, tiny paper horses, pictures, delicately colored candies—and flowers, innumerable flowers: sewn into garlands, woven, arranged, bound together, displayed luxuriously or sparely; we never stopped crushing them as we walked on, and their perfume overwhelmed all other smells of the bazaar. The fabric boutiques looked like rays of the sun broken by a prism. Antique dealers displayed magic chests from Siam, little balls to amuse birds, shadowplay theatres shaped like chimeras, Chinese hats, an amputee-incubus, worn-out games of Literature and Vanity. At the market's far end, a bookstall was run by der-vishes. In great red copper cauldrons, priests stirred up innumerable tiny gods of yellow cop-per, and they rattled around the vats like hail. And there a civil servant (in a silk robe embroi-dered with little fat men playing blindman's bluff) overtook us, pursued us, and as we ran, the crowd kept shoving us back. When he caught us we were thrown into a palanquin and carried off to the local prison.

They locked me alone in a cell, and I was plunged into despair. "Will I ever see you again, towns folded around vast bays like dead birds' wings? You ocean cities atop great promontories like sentinels?" Yes, I was tired of my Mediterranean island, where bearded old men repair decaying galleys that sink slowly in the harbor ooze, stuck there in a panorama of red seawalls, ruins, and sun-faded masts. Joylessly I used to go see the foreigners who had taken over the rundown hotels of ship owners. Nearly motionless, penetrated by the languor and calm of the setting sun, they were ageless beings, immortal as the mermaids brought back from Japan, or as the small frigates nailed to the wall, all busy with sails. The Red Ones sat between two horned skulls, surprisingly frail, pale eyes…the Black Ones danced in front of bonfires, throwing exaggerated shadows onto the sea… I preferred instead the galleys of the old port, the ships stuck like me in spangled mud, in a gloomy life, mottled with tortoiseshell light. The heavy seas no longer tossed those ships about; dappled rats and slime-green rats traced signs with their tails in the dust of years. Squirrels and shrew-mice romped along their rigging; curious tapirs, intelligent, sniffed the portholes; ostriches no bigger than chickens walked in tandem on the deck; owls in revolt against their race held frivolous conversations that made them grow golden feathers. In the darkness of the cabins and corridors, large cats passed among heaps of jewels and stacks of drowsing tortoises; through the round windows the sunken white statue and the seahorse spied on these feline phantoms... Beneath the town, underground passages dug by Those of the Ancient Religions extended in all directions; salted away throughout were small mummies of alligators. Here and there scarabs wandered, the phosphorescent eyes of sacred cats sewn up into shrouds...

And as I left all this behind, I thought: Oh seas of Asia, I yearn for the pale light of the medusas that drift on your warm tides, for the fickle galleys trapped by black coral reefs, for fish hovering motionless above the chained

skeletons of oarsmen... Barks and vessels of the
Orient, your scent rests in my heart, my old
man's heart which has surrendered none of itself,
and which does not know whether this slight
trembling in the hands is age or desire...

"Wake up, man! You're about to appear
before the prince of this country, the one known
as the Little Mogul."

He reposed, surrounded by barbaric
princes decked out in small trembling feathers,
and in the shadows he caressed monsters with
soft fur while he listened to his messengers.

"Prince, I went to Babylon the Deserted,
as you asked. The town lies in dust, and the
hanging gardens of Semiramis have collapsed."

"That's fine. I will go further, much further. Do you know Hell? Hell with its sky full of
violet stars, forsaken fires atop its high cliffs, and
solemn songs in its depths?"

"Prince, the sorcerers of the archipelago
know the dry scent of the fires of Hell, where
your subjects weep. They know how processions
march, seared by blinding flames from herb-filled
braziers. Storks and heavy demons fly through

the red smoke, and the damned souls fall thick as dead beasts. There are no songs there, Prince."

"There are songs, I tell you, solemn music. Have you nothing more to report?"

"In the furthest forests of your domain, bleached bones of dragons shine with black insects, and the sun rises through dragon carcasses, laying striped shadows across the desert..."

"And you, Idekel?"

"My Prince, I have guided your daughter to the fish-eating tsar. I have seen hills covered with blissful castles, plains where debonair lions promenade, and a level and lonely horizon where herds of elephants pursue tigers, the tigers pursue succulent unicorns, all these running through living whirlwinds of sand. I have seen rivers fall from Paradise, with a sound like whole forests rustling—then the plains grooved by heavy rains—then snow, snow, and more snow—finally the clinking relics of the princess, just that one sound, crucified throughout the immense Christian night. Finally, one morning on the far side of a river that was busy carting away triangular chunks of ice, we saw their bearded little black

sentinels up in the bare trees, and they launched
a boat to meet us, laden with scarlet swine, gifts of
the tsar... And the town, with its cold meals, its
log cabins jammed together like wood lice, its
timber palace..."

"And then?"

"Tsar, I said, please accept these gifts from
my master. Accept these rare crimson koi, these
pebbles that come alive at night like eyes, these
salamanders that secrete a cloth that fire will
anneal. Accept these riches I have laid out before
you, and also this young fatted empress..."

"You have done well."

"The tsar fixed me with his stare, a fish
tail in his hands. The fish head between his teeth
had its eyes still open; a tiny fish was tangled in
his beard. The sub-chieftains brought in more
bleeding hunks of flesh, on hooks...And the idols,
sweaty, upright, were red as the meat. A plaque
made of fish bones glimmered on the Grand
Sorcerer's chest; the princess was afraid of the
Eternal Genie of the Snow... Soft pale blue
clouds rose from the town: offerings to the gods
of the wind..."

"Tell me more."

"I heard the war chant of a savage chieftain who'd been caught and thrown into a vat of serpents. He died singing, his hands clutching vipers like broken fetters. And the wind brought me the laughter of the flat-faced spectators."

"But the princess?"

"Every morning without fail, great silver-filigreed chimeras floated from that horizon the color of ice. Silent invasions were being planned … At the command of the princess, all the gods of the conquered tribes were chained up, one by one, in a cave filled with large millipedes… One day the temple caught fire; the blackened gods came forth. The tsar's guards fought with blue axes against masses of rebel horsemen, who brandished the greased skulls of great beasts…"

"And now?"

"Now the tsarina rules by herself. During winter thaw she sent the final gods down the river like ponderous boats. (There's now a huge cemetery of these at the mouth of the river.) From the palace the Tsarina showed this deathly flotilla to the captive gods of the tribute states, the mildewing gods whose chains she herself had fastened to the bars of the windows while the Christian priests sang…"

"And you, messenger in green, what have you to tell me?"

"We burn forests to harvest magic charms; the plum-skinned demons fly off snickering; homesick ambassadors approach, sleepwalking, and scatter the fallen angels in their diadems of gray stars…"

"Homesick? For what towns?"

"Towns where beasts gravitate, silent and slow as deep-sea creatures, translucent, revolving around the black palm trees; where the breeze brings the clatter of shells that decorate the gazelles of savages; where high limbless trees undulate in the wind like ocean kelp. A town known for its parades, whose inhabitants beg your help in fighting off huge flocks of birds with butterfly markings, birds that have chased them from their homes, and now sleep in rows on the blackened village walls…"

"Enough, enough, messenger. Like the tattooed kings of the islands, from now on I'll only collect talkative dwarves, little jesters to amuse."

He closed his eyes. The messengers withdrew. Then he began to dictate, to his white-bearded secretary, a letter in Persian:

How could I ever forget you, Princess of China? You appeared to me above twenty cities of asphalt and clay, cities that clawed at the buffeting yellow wind. In the distance, a black river snaked between two pheasantcolored hills. Covered with a blaze of kingfisher feathers, you made me dream of the girls who play their flutes beside the tombs of your country, so full of grace! And made me think of those wise men who tear out their flower gardens to replace them with a perfect lawn where, all by itself, a single autumn crocus blooms. In autumn you drape the valleys with russet furs, valleys suddenly populated by exotic deer; you give us steppes around abandoned tombs, and lay as a funeral offering the Michaelmas daisy that grows high on the slopes, haunted by shrew-mice. Smooth glossy fruits: mango, mangosteen, Japanese persimmon; manyseeded fruits: lemon, orange, grapefruit; lightly-downed fruits: litchi; hairy fruits: pineapple and sugar cane, cleverly arranged—all these form your barbarous, vegetal throne. In

Kashmir, the traders think of you when they buy their butterfly-patterned lizards; the natives of the archipelago know that you dance like a child at the center of a large rose window, while fragments of colored light race around the chamber like cats. And when I have neglected you for a few days, I return to find you, faithful, under a sky filled with braids of hair, where thousands of tiny hands suddenly open up and fly toward the South, in a mysterious exodus...

He turned toward me. "Talk to me about the Princess of China."

I had never seen her.

"Ah! Weariness," sighed the prince, "weariness. Neither have I, you poor thing." And, after a moment of silence:

"Give him to the army."

*

So I was taken to the army. I was given the post of Historian to the Prince, and was pressed into the next campaign. The Prince, who had just extirpated the Persian army, sent us to conquer

the undefended Ispahan. I wrote my story with
the help of a messenger named Idekel: an old
man, sweet-tempered, who had followed the last
expedition and who kept a grave expression as he
told me his life:

"It's worthless," he said, "a youth spent in
scholarship—I was initiated very young; by
thirty I was a magician. I took part in the War
Against the Demons, which occurred during the
reign of King Abbas. I journeyed with all the
other magicians to the islands of Hell. I saw
young demons who had just cut off their horns as
a sign of emancipation, and the old ones, covered
with subtle tattoos and wrinkles, which looked
like ancient cracked faiences. I saw the damned
file along through snow, like lines of miserable
ants, escorted by fluttering demons. They advanced toward the horizon until they reached the
mines; some of them escaped by jumping onto
phantom ships. Some of us had learned powerful
secret spells by reading the constellations of this
hemisphere—spells you concoct by throwing tiny
dusty roses, those Tartarus roses with the over-
powering scent, into the blood of sirens. Legions
of demons fled us. We watched them form into

triangular flocks like migrating birds; they would slowly orient themselves, then take off for other continents. People in the countryside later caught them with snares, used pikes to finish them off. (But some of these demons survived, and now live in a thin and pitiful state in the Buddha-decorated caverns around Samarkand. Their fluttering has degenerated into heavy, slow flapping, and onlookers think they're watching giant bats...)

"But not all the demons were killed. I don't really know how it is that they managed to conquer us in the end. For several weeks, I couldn't walk out my front door a single morning without finding famous magicians hung, one after another, from the trees along the promenade used by the kings of Irkenise (which is where I lived after my return from the infernal islands). In their magician's garb, gaunt with death, they were a magnificent spectacle: sun sparkled on their peaked hats and on their robes embroidered with castles and rearing lions... As for me, I forbade myself the use of sorcery for a long time, but in vain. Bit by bit I forgot my conscience; I was indifferent to learning, teaching, everything.

Bizarre daze was all I wanted: staring at the sun or being hypnotized by flickering fire. I'm no drunkard, I smoke very little and use hashish only in moderation. But I soon degenerated...and I woke up one day to find myself in the army, a passive derelict thrown in among violent derelicts...

"You are not young, but I'll bet you've never seen a proper conflagration. A real conflagration, that's one of the most perfect works of God. A fire like that enchants everything it touches; its thick radiating light carves the deepest shadows.

"So listen: we took the palace of Ispahan by four o'clock...the Persian soldiers had gorgeous weapons, but we slit their throats anyway. That night we all met up again in the palace garden with food, wine, and our precious loot, and we feasted; it was all shouting and the clatter of silver and gold. An hour after nightfall we heard they'd broken into the underground vaults. Some of the men with me spoke later of a great rumbling. That's not true, no. There was no such sound. We just suddenly found ourselves standing there, one of us holding an old-fashioned water

jug by the handle, a roast chicken leg being held
by another, faces astounded, bewildered—all at
once we were rushing toward the palace. Its
grandiose doors were already surrounded by
troops. All the elite regiments had gathered there,
seized by the same frenzy. Every soldier fought
every other; the fights kept starting but never got
finished because no one had the time to brood
over his honor. And just then the conflagration
erupted. I saw it clearly, because my diffidence
had kept me well back from the doors. Fire
moved slowly across the rooftops, like a beast,
small crackling flames of mauve and russet. To
the perfume I'd thought was roses, but was really
the scent of the expansive gardens covered with
mountain snow, was now added the smell of
charring... Men came out of the palace carrying
armfuls of magnificent objects covered with silk
and pearls: automata, richly-dressed oversize
dolls, ancient toys... These soldiers were Afghan
and Tadzhik troops, the most savage contingent of
the army; they advanced slowly, hallucinating,
making a low muttering that grew into an uproar:
'The gods! The gods! THE GODS!' For hundreds
of years the masters of the ports had picked out a

tithe of the rarest objects arriving from the
subjugated nations, and delivered them up to the
throne. Certain rooms in the underground vault
were blanketed in ash, cinders of the century's
most beautiful flowers and rarest fruits. Upstairs,
innumerable toys, tumbled together, filled chamber after chamber, receding into the inner dis-
tances of the palace: the princes of this dynasty
had acquired a hereditary taste for such playthings. For over three centuries, the kings of
earth had respectfully propitiated these childish,
difficult desires.

"But now, to escape the melee, soldiers
huddled together and lifted the trophies they
carried above their heads. The automata, dolls,
and mechanical animals advanced slowly, dark,
catching none of the light from the conflagration,
though it was now intense as the gleam within the
dolls' false jewels.

"This night was certainly one of the great-
est nights in the history of the world, one of those
nights when the stunned gods surrender the earth
to the savage demons of poetry. All night, you
understand, all night in a long farandole, these
hirsute soldiers spun around the blazing palace

and campfires, shouting, gingerly holding these
delicate toys, which caressed one another as they
passed; the soldiers finally became disoriented in
the plundered gardens until their cries were
masked by the sounds of flutes and hurdy-
gurdies... In shadows far from the blaze, execu-
tioners and Chinese archers carried off in their
cupped hands the real pearls of the fallen
princes, to sell them in the kingdoms of the South,
where the kings all paint their bodies...

"I had been impatient to leave. By the
second day of marching my astonishment was
infinite. I had seen our armies in the old days: the
ranks kept good formation and marched cor-
rectly. But this night we walked any which way,
wearing whatever, scarcely armed. Sometimes
elegant officers, their turbans topped with long
egret plumes, capered among us on their swan-
necked steeds, then took off again, proud of
themselves no doubt. And we advanced into the
desert like a thick fog tinted orange or violet,
walled in on all sides, sometimes encountering
savage mountain peaks where images of solemn
kings had once been engraved, and had indicated
with their fingers routes now forgotten. We even-

tually came upon villages: a blue cupola over walls of rectangular clay, silhouettes of palm trees, and a well surrounded by majestic tombs of a disappeared race. Many of the soldiers had brought tame animals along; when it came time to decamp they looked for them in vain, and then just left.

"Emperor Basil II, whom we historians call the Bulgaroctone, he called me Idekel. He had countless Bulgarian prisoners blinded. He ranged these blind soldiers in ranks of ten; they held each other by the hand, then he gave them an eleventh prisoner from whom he had torn only one eye. Thus the army which had vowed to overrun Byzantium returned to Bulgaria, in biting cold, through savage mountains and barren fields. For centuries afterward one could trace this army's route by the endless lines of graves of the blind soldiers: tall gravestones carved, like targets, with wide-open eyes. Prince Vlad of Transylvania, at the time of his great retreat, hung Turkish corpses high in the trees. Many years later, when the sultan's troops were again ready to invade, they would be forced to advance through endless trees garnished with skeletons, in which vultures and storks had made their nests from dead branches larger than rib bones; rusted swords hung there... We left behind us a less savage legacy; our path will become sanctified. The villages where we stopped will be easy to recognize, thanks to the domesticated animals of all sorts, which—due to the negligence of our soldiers—are already established there. With their endless pranks, little gray monkeys perched on walls everyplace will let travelers know where we camped. The fast-multiplying parakeets will invade the countryside; the frogs and mongooses will docilely follow old men, and the children who play at village gates will be surrounded by circles of intelligent, attentive rabbits..." Certainly we lost many animals. Good taste, which led our officers to daydream of their lovers and forget about their troops, had not disappeared: a charming liberty reigned, and by the time we reached the outskirts of Ispahan the provisions were nearly exhausted, even after we'd lightly pillaged the Armenian city. At the center of a circle of mountains as blue as illuminated letters in a medieval manuscript, Ispahan rested in a mist that filled its gardens. Then we saw countless cupolas even bluer than the mountains; high up there, storks described vast patterns in a sky drained of all color. Before us, the walls still stood, walls of ancient earthen houses that had fallen to dust. Crenellated fragments of wall stood in the fields like vestigial Roman aqueducts; an immense bridge with pointed arches dominated a ravine at the bottom of which flowed only an unseen stream. We crossed it and set up our encampment in the outskirts of the city. We didn't raise tents: the houses were abandoned. After the last invasion, the population had dropped to sixty thousand. It had once boasted a population of over eight hundred thousand; this Muslim city with only low buildings was more spread-out than Amsterdam, Genoa, or Venice. The inhabitants who remained had taken refuge in the center of the city, leaving the other, surrounding quarters deserted. Many different species of animals took possession of those abandoned quarters. When we tried to capture some sheep for our evening meal, we found packs that fled before us down the dusty roads, stray dogs half-wild. The orders came soon to bed down for the night—because next morning we would have to make a triumphant, worthy march through the center of town and the famous parade ground created long ago at the behest of Abbas the Great.

Next morning, we didn't hear the thin wooden horns sound their call. We passed a restful, refreshing morning in a languor that was made all the more precious by the ambience of one of the most beautiful cities in the world. The beige walls had such fine tint; the blue sky reflected off the white lime cupolas. Purple flowers, whose name I don't know, close-set as leaves on trees, fell from the roofs to earth, covering the facades and filling up the windowframes till they blocked the view. A hand suddenly wiped these away: where we expected the veiled face of a woman, instead there appeared the homely head of an Indian or a black man with a wide smile. We searched the houses, lit their dark corners with torches and dug under their mildewed divans. And didn't we find every last scrap? The jewelry of poor people, household gods cast in lead, moth-eaten clothes, books. One fellow found a mirror at the bottom of a hole, left it there and went to eat lunch; on his return he found in place of the mirror a rat that fled squealing. Another soldier found splendid drawings that included lyre-birds and striped genies. I found nothing. After the siesta, I saw men gathering and whispering together. I approached this group and learned that they still hadn't found the gates to the city.

Before our arrival, the inhabitants (who could no longer hope to fight us since they no longer had an army) had constructed a thousand small walls which had blocked all the gates and turned the town into a labyrinth; they disguised their work so well that we weren't able to distinguish old walls from new ones. We broke up laughing when we saw this eccentric defense, and to amuse ourselves went around smashing walls at random. Again, evening lengthened the shadows, which rose to claim the forms of indifferent storks perched in the branches.

The next morning I woke at sunrise and climbed to a rooftop to get a view of the quarter where we had set up camp. Everything looked strangely pink. It seemed it wasn't a matter of sunrise coloring the chalk-white houses, but rather that someone had painted them in the night. But little by little they came back to their white color. And pink lizards, whichhad gathered by the millions in abandoned caves, came out now to spread across the countryside and throughout the city, as the sun rose...

A few hours passed; I remained sprawled out on the roof, conquering cities in my daydreams. When I came back down, some of my companions were dead. They had been stung by scorpions. I heard that some horses had also been killed.

Already the animals that had fled at our arrival were losing their fear of us, and were returning. Dogs launched themselves down every street, shooting between the legs of soldiers and knocking them down like dolls. Cats—clever animals—stole our food. Sometimes at a streetcorner we saw the melancholy silhouette of a camel without its master. We killed the dogs and cats. The other animals disappeared.

But our provisions were running out. Soldiers demolished the walls after having spied from the rooftops the location of the town center, but, lacking the right equipment, they had to hack at the walls with their weapons, and progressed slowly. Night returned with its cortege of constellations and black scorpions; more soldiers died.

A few days passed this way. Our triumph drew near but we were starving. The dogs and cats, terrified, fled as soon as they saw us: we couldn't catch them. Those we had killed earlier we now found full of scorpions. All that carrion drew these arachnids, and soon every night brought us fear of new assaults. We took to living on the roofs, playing cards and telling stories, because we had already drunk all our wine. Sometimes we heard a faint song or the jingling of a donkey's bells drift up from town...what tedium...

Thus the demons of the ruins were born, who are faceless and live in our own bodies. (No doubt one of these demons is born in every one of us.) Mine was loquacious but eloquent. At the hour of the siesta, when the sun made fleeting, dangerous mirages rise from the sand of the street and the burning walls, or when poisonous night brought the accustomed terror, this demon spoke to me slowly. And it said: "You remember the towns of gunny sacks, of sheet metal and gray sludge, from which antelopes stream forth, led along salt marshes by tall black herdsmen whose

spearheads gleam—those towns where severed
heads have just bled dry at the center of a blazing
square, under a leafless tree heavy with wading
birds—those cities with muddy arroyos that are
lined on the right banks with Chinese merchants
of monsters, and on the left banks with all the
birds of the islands—those cities where boards
falling in the bazaar sound like gunshots, and the
noise brings creatures running out of huge abandoned pagodas that reflect in the river's spangled
surface, while invisible mosquitoes drone—those
cities where tropical dawn awakens sonorous
canals, reawakening the goldsmiths, reanimating
the hammering of foils and cheap trinkets, and on
the waterways a flowering of small boats that pass
each other with great nonchalance, piled high
with spongy pink fruits—those cities always
besieged by armies, filled with dust clouds, tumul-
tuous, the starry skies reflecting in war shields,
dominated by the pinnacles of pale temples—
those cities that resemble barbarian camps,
founded by setting carts upside-down at the
bends of wide rivers bordered with coconut
palms, under a huge birdless sky—you remember
those cities peopled by men in turbans who all

along the harbor sell great bronze peacocks that
are actually demons (obscene cities)—those cities
ruled by old gods with many arms, their gilt
chipping off, tottering, where the old men with
grave disquieted eyes stare at stuffed bears
brought from Europe that have taken the place of
family gods—those cities whose walls are made of
the interlocked horns of beasts, and where one
can find a singing tree—you still remember those
cities where the towers are pearl-divers, where
bodies climb slowly, half in fog, heavy with the
dreams of an entire sleeping race—you recall
those cities of grand festivals, where all the sweet
playthings from near and far, old and new, having
died, come back to life in electric twilight—those
cities where an obscure people blossoms under
the scepter of Estragon the Fifth, attended by his
cats Gryphon, Mustachio and Freckles—those
cities whose sensitive citizens spend their for-
tunes on bright white firework displays, competi-
tions involving fish that change color like chame-
leons, and choirs of musical kites that sing like
Aeolian harps—those cities that have mastered
the occult sciences, their dead wearing masks of
darkest silver—you remember those cities where

musical notes, filled with blue light, flutter and hum at night, and when they collide explode in the purest sound—those cities that are made of enormous blocks of crystal, through which all the colors of the rainbow flicker like huge birds— finally, you remember those cities whose houses look like serene faces, though after dusk their chimney smoke sends sea urchins, mauve sturgeons and phosphorescent cyprinoids up to the moon. But you won't remember Ispahan, because Ispahan belongs to the beasts. Its crown of desolation will protect it from your cursed comrades and their vile officers. Nothing can defeat those born in sand; their image rules among all the constellations. Vain to try to understand their dark restlessness…"

Idekel, too, was listening to a demon, who said: "Do you know an army has gathered in the South to defend Ispahan? You must flee to the East. In the East are towns like rich men's dreams, where demons live idle and heedless. If you go to Golconda, sorcerer, you'll be hung. But you will not go to Golconda; before you see the high palm trees of the Indies, you will encounter salt deserts. Their crystalline surfaces gleam like frost, and there is no more beautiful backdrop for a lone skeleton, abandoned beside traces of a campfire on a nearly invisible trail. Dream of your death, artist."

When evening came we recited to each other the words of our demons; our whispering was almost the only sound. Every soldier heard the voice that rose up within him, and was shattered by it. And when the runaway camels of a nomad king crossed through our camp with beards of seashells, and foxtails stuck to their ears, no one lifted a finger. The jingling of their tiny bells faded; the army fell back into its deep sleep like a single body sinking in hibernation...

The city defended itself: most of the men were killed by scorpions, or fled into the desert. Probably by now vultures were approaching the bodies, which lay in sand among tufts of aromatic moss.

One evening I had such dread of the oncoming night, I decided not to sleep at all. I headed toward the officers' quarters. Not a soul was there. A shadow hurried along the alley; atop the dark figure rose a plume that reflected the starlight, and I was able to follow.

We walked a long time. We went through narrow passageways, between walls whose undulating uneven ridges looked in the dark like they had been gnawed by some ancient beast that lived among fire-worshippers. We crossed deserted squares, their geometric outlines lost to sight under dust. And we ended up in the countryside, along the grand avenue of King Abbas, with its willows and its mosaic palace.

Silence! Silence! The light warm wind broke off bits of the mosaics; pomegranate and sweetbrier were in bloom; other flowers, still invisible, scented the night air. In the long pools that lined the avenue, marvelous fish brought here by Tamerlane unscrolled their tails amid starlight on the waters. It seemed as if mankind had disappeared from the earth, and that plants, silent animals, and stones lived in the perfect liberty that follows upon hopeless abandonment. The officer I was following approached one of the statues that lined the pools. It stood up and followed him! Stupefied, I looked more closely: the gray masses here and there were not statues but men. I walked beside the pools, hidden by shrubs, and in the light mist our silk-clad officers, hungry as the rest of us, were fishing in those pools for hundred-year-old fish...

When I returned to camp in the morning, after my night of oblivion, the mercenaries of the Ganges were gathered again around a pyre on which they were burning the dead. The last few hours had been particularly lethal, and we realized we would not break through to the town center for a very long time... The men watched the black smoke rise, breathing in its terrible thick stench, their jaws clenched, penetrated by a disgust and a despair so absolute they no longer even thought of getting into quarrels. The horses never stopped whinnying. Dogs and cats that had fled us the night before, sunken in horror like us, now dashed across the camp. Intrigued, I climbed up onto a flat roof.

The town was calm: around the mosques flew pigeons and turtledoves. But the ruins that the fleeing lizards had previously tinted pink were black this morning, absolutely black. Disturbed, I pushed myself up on an elbow, then stood. At once I understood both the terror of the animals we'd seen rushing past, and the meaning of this large blot that now advanced on us. Flab-

bergasted, I shouted "Scorpions! Scorpions!"
Everyone rushed for the roofs. In minutes, this
word and the spectacle of the immense insect
sheet fringed with pincers so horrified us that our
army shattered in a vast whirlwind, carrying off
officers and princes as the terror drove us out of
the city in a welter of arms, of clamor, of horses
screaming. Madness suddenly seized the whole
multitude of troops, and threw them by handfuls
like grains of sand out to the vultures of the
desert.

*

I will never know how I reached
Trebizond. I remember hunger and thirst, and
the bells of a camel caravan in the North that
rescued me, to the accompaniment of bellowing
frogs. Camel herders in string-wound turbans
nursed me; I arrived here dazed, senseless,
guarded by children covered with amulets. The
prince took me in; everywhere in the world the
only talk was of our defeat. I hardly knew how to
talk about it. It was beyond me. But I've managed
to make a living selling beautiful shells. Some-

times I'm defenseless against my memory of that
town surrounded by blue mountains, my
memory of that morning when our army surrendered its scattering troops to solitude, like burnt
offerings, while black smoke of a sacrificial pyre
rose above the ramparts… Only winter frees
me… When the Black Sea wind begins to blow
cold through the village, I stay indoors; for days
I exhaust myself brooding over the incompre-
hensible shapes of seashells. (There are shells
that communicate with demons in hell, but
nobody knows it.) I bought ancient foreign
objects. How perfectly they hold their tongues! I
converse with them the way Idekel spoke with
the fire. I've also acquired two sirens; I will sell
them to the prince. His Christian minister tells
him sirens do not exist; he is wrong. They do
exist: a butterfly collector who has become my
friend has seen them. He whispered that his
were not exactly like mine, which were no doubt
fashioned in Korea from the heads and arms of
small mummified monkeys grafted to the bodies
of fish. But the prince believes in sirens, because
he wants to possess them. With the money he will
give me, maybe I'll book passage on one of the

ships that sail to the Fortune Islands. I'm only
sixty years old...